The Water Hole

Additional copies may be ordered from the publisher for educational,
business, promotional or premium use.
For information, contact ALIVE Book Publishing at:
alivebookpublishing.com, or call (925) 837-7303.

ISBN 13
978-1-63132-107-8 Hardcover
978-1-63132-108-5 Paperback

Library of Congress Control Number: 2020919138

Library of Congress Cataloging-in-Publication Data
is available upon request.

First Edition

Published in the United States of America by ALIVE Book Publishing
and ALIVE Publishing Group, imprints of Advanced Publishing LLC
3200 A Danville Blvd., Suite 204, Alamo, California 94507
alivebookpublishing.com

PRINTED IN THE UNITED STATES OF AMERICA

10 9 8 7 6 5 4 3 2 1

The Water Hole

Written by
Corrin Haskell

Illustrated by Andre Jones

ABOOKS
Alive Book Publishing

At some point in time, a baby elephant was born in the Eastern part of Africa. He was a normal looking elephant, but just smaller because he was a baby.

He had grey, tough skin; four legs with four knees; a tail; big, floppy ears; and a long nose called a trunk. They named him "Boomie."

As the elephant grew up, he learned how elephants survive. He learned how to communicate and sense danger. He learned how to find food and water. He was even taught how to give himself a nice mud bath.

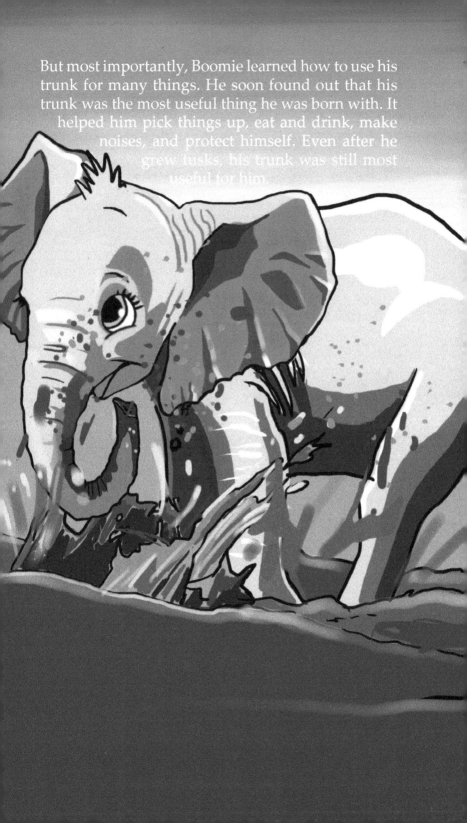

But most importantly, Boomie learned how to use his trunk for many things. He soon found out that his trunk was the most useful thing he was born with. It helped him pick things up, eat and drink, make noises, and protect himself. Even after he grew tusks, his trunk was still most useful for him.

He spent his days traveling across the plains of Africa with the rest of the elephant herd. They passed the time sleeping, eating, and walking; sleeping, eating, and walking; sleeping, eating, and walking. Every now and then, they would meet other elephants and talk about "elephant things" with them. As time went on, the baby elephant grew bigger and bigger.

The bigger he became, the more he could do. Soon, he grew tired of the "elephant-way-of-life": sleeping, eating, and walking; sleeping, eating, and walking; sleeping, eating, and walking.

"Surely there must be more to life than just sleeping, eating and walking," he thought.

So one day, Boomie decided to leave the herd and go on a little adventure by himself.

"I will go to the waterhole alone today, for I am big enough now to do things on my own," he said to himself.

This little elephant had been taught well by his parents, so he had no fear when he set out for the waterhole alone for the first time. He left very early in the morning, as everyone was still sleeping and would not notice him.

There are many dangers out in the wild that a young elephant has to look out for. There are other animals who may want to attack you; you must know the right things to eat so you don't get sick; you could lose your way and get lost in the vast African plains.

But the elephant had been warned that the greatest danger to all the animals was a creature named, "*MAN.*"

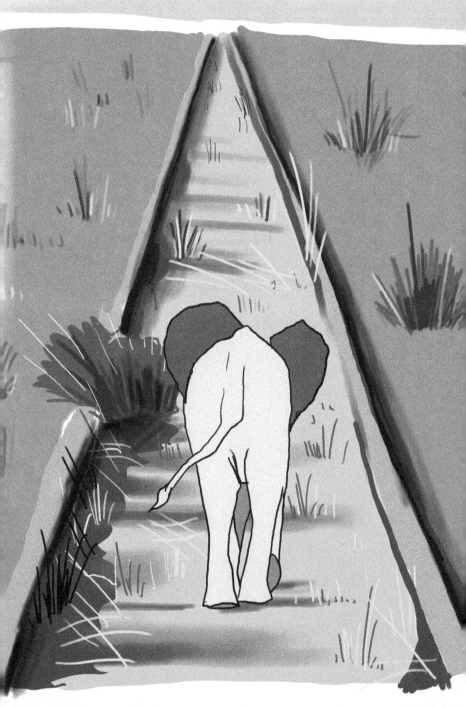

Suddenly, the elephant saw a group of these *men* with big sticks talking near the waterhole. He sat low in the tall grass, as he'd been taught to do, so he would not be seen.

The elephant had been told that *men* just like these had killed some of his relatives. So he stayed low in the grass, and soon the men got into a metal beast and went away.

As he reached the waterhole, he did not see any other elephants. Instead, he saw many other animals, all who looked quite different from him. He saw a spotted animal with a neck so long, that his head could reach up the top of the highest tree to eat grass. He saw a big, fat animal with a huge mouth who was

making a lot of noise. He saw a green animal, with short arms and legs, swimming underneath the water.

"What a weird group of animals," he thought to himself. Much different than the elephants he was used to.

As he approached the waterhole, Boomie noticed that the other animals stopped what they were doing and looked at him. Suddenly the hippo asked him, "What happened to your nose? Why is it so long?"

"Yeah," the giraffe said, "I can't tell if it's a nose or a tail." All of them laughed. "And his ears," said the alligator, "they look like the wings of a bird. Can you use them to fly?" Again, they all laughed at him.

The elephant felt strange. He had never seen creatures like this, much less talked to them. His parents had told him not to go around other animals because elephants were supposed to stay together and look after each other.

"Well, can you talk," asked the Hippo, "or does that nose cover up your mouth?" All of them laughed again.

Eventually the elephant began to feel sad. He did not like being laughed at. As his long nose hung down in the water, he began to cry. As he did this, his nose began to fill up with water. All of a sudden, Boomie the elephant let go a big sneeze.

"AAA-CHOOOOO!" He accidently sprayed the giraffe with a lot of water.

While the other animals laughed, the giraffe was very upset.

"You have gotten my beautiful, spotted fur all wet,"
he said. And he threw a coconut at the little elephant.
The other animals seemed to get extremely excited.
"Spray me! Me next!" they began to yell. The giraffe
still looked very upset.

As the elephant began to spray the other animals with water, he heard a familiar voice say, "Boomie, what are you doing?"

It was his parents and the rest of the elephants from the herd. "We have been looking all over for you.

Why are you playing with these other creatures? We elephants must stay together so that we will be safe and able to survive."

"What you are teaching this little one is not right!" said a big, deep voice. All of a sudden, a great lion came out of the tall grasses. It was Musa, the Lion

King of Africa. All the animals stopped what they were doing, and listened to the great Lion King speak.

"It is not wise for us animals to stay separated in different tribes any longer," Musa said, "For these days we have a new, common danger that we face. We must now work together and use the different skills we have to help each other survive."

"What is this new danger you speak of?" one of the elephants asked. "This new danger is called *Man*. The creature is trying to control the land so they can have everything they think they need to survive. Surely, you have noticed that our lands are getting smaller; there is not as much food as in the past; *Man* will even kill you for your body parts, or just for fun,"

explained Musa. "But why does *Man* hurt us? We have not troubled him in any way?" the giraffe asked. "We animals stand in the way. *Man* wants all of the land for himself and destroys anything that is in the way. We animals must come together in order to survive," Musa explained.

The animals understood the great King's wisdom and saw that they could no longer stay separated in tribes. The elephants, and other animals, agreed that there is strength in numbers and decided to unite. They spent the rest of the day getting to know each other and playing in the water hole.

About the Author & Illustrator

Corrin Haskell has been teaching at Brookfield Elementary in Oakland, California, for 25 years. Born and raised in Seattle, he moved to California in the mid-nineties to pursue a teaching career after graduating from the University of Washington. He founded and ran the reggae/dancehall record label, Lion Kings Productions, for two decades before moving into the world of children's literature. The Water Hole is his debut publication. It is the first of many children's books he has written and hopes to release in the coming years.

Oakland resident Andre Jones is a muralist, designer, and executive director of the Bay Area Mural Program. His illustrative style under the alias, "Natty Rebel," has landed him projects from East Oakland to East Africa. He holds a B.A. in commercial art from Virginia Commonwealth University and considers himself am "Art Anthropologist." His mission is to employ the visual arts to inspire and redesign urban communities.

ALIVE Book Publishing and ALIVE Publishing Group are imprints of Advanced Publishing LLC, 3200 A Danville Blvd., Suite 204, Alamo, California 94507 Telephone: 925.837.7303   alivebookpublishing.com

ABOOKS